Going Batty

For Jane O'Connor, with thanks for all she does for Katie and me.—NK

For Jonas, head honcho of the bat cave.—J&W

ISBN-13: 978-0-545-21014-0
ISBN-10: 0-545-21014-3

Text copyright © 2009 by Nancy Krulik.
Illustrations copyright © 2009 by John and Wendy.
All rights reserved. Published by Scholastic Inc., 557 Broadway, New York, NY 10012, by arrangement with Grosset & Dunlap, a division of Penguin Young Readers Group, a member of Penguin Group (USA) Inc. SCHOLASTIC and associated logos are trademarks and/or registered trademarks of Scholastic Inc.

12 11 10 9 8 7 6 5 4 3 2 1   9 10 11 12 13 14/0

Printed in the U.S.A.   40

First Scholastic printing, September 2009

Katie Kazoo

SWITCHEROO

Going Batty

by Nancy Krulik • illustrated by John & Wendy

SCHOLASTIC INC.
New York Toronto London Auckland
Sydney Mexico City New Delhi Hong Kong

Chapter 1

"I love seeing things upside down," Katie Carew said as she flipped over on the monkey bars. "Everyone looks so funny."

"I know," Katie's best friend, Suzanne Lock, agreed. "It's like they're walking on the ceiling."

"A *cement* ceiling," Katie added with a giggle.

Just then, Becky Stern scrambled up the monkey bars. She hooked her knees over one of the metal bars, and flipped upside down next to Katie and Suzanne.

"Hi, Becky," Katie greeted her.

"Yeah, hi," Suzanne added. She didn't sound as happy to see Becky as Katie did.

"I'm wearing shorts under my skirt so no one can see my underpants," Becky told the girls.

"I've been wearing shorts under my skirts since second grade," Suzanne said proudly. "I was the first one in the whole school to do it. But you wouldn't know that because you didn't move here until the middle of *third* grade."

Katie rolled her eyes. That was *soooo*

Suzanne. She was always bragging.

"You know, when we smile it looks like we're frowning," Becky told Katie and Suzanne. "At least to the people who are standing right-side up."

Suzanne frowned. Katie could tell it was a real frown because she and Suzanne were both upside down. Suzanne looked right-side up to her. Well, sort of.

Katie knew exactly why Suzanne was frowning. Becky had changed the subject. Suzanne hated not being the center of attention.

Just then Katie spotted her other best friend, Jeremy Fox, walking by with George Brennan and Kevin Camilleri. Now no matter what Suzanne said or did, Becky wouldn't pay any attention to her. That was because Becky had a crush on Jeremy. A *huge* crush.

Unfortunately, Jeremy did *not* have a crush on Becky. He usually tried to stay far, far away from her. But Becky had seen Jeremy. There was no way he could avoid her now.

"Hi, Jeremy!" Becky called out.

Jeremy pushed his glasses up on his nose and looked down at the ground. "Hi, Becky," he muttered.

George and Kevin laughed.

"Hi, Jeremy," George said, making his voice sound high and squeaky, like a girl's.

"Cut it out," Jeremy told George.

"Your *girlfriend* is calling you," Kevin joked.

"She is *not* my girlfriend!" Jeremy insisted.

"Watch this, Jeremy!" Becky shouted. She grabbed hold of the bars on either side of her. Then she flipped over, and flew off the monkey bars. She landed on her feet and threw her arms up in the air.

"Awesome," George said.

"Very cool," Kevin added.

"Did you like my flip, Jeremy?" Becky asked him.

Jeremy shrugged. "It was okay," he said. Then he ran off as fast as he could.

Suzanne sat up on the monkey bars. Katie did, too. "Becky's such a show-off," Suzanne whispered to Katie. "I am so sick of her doing gymnastics all the time! And I hate the way she always copies me. She didn't have to wear a skirt with shorts under it. She could have worn jeans, like you."

Katie sighed. Suzanne was just mad because everyone had thought Becky's flip was really cool.

"I'm sorry Becky ever moved here," Suzanne said. "I wish she would just go back to where she came from!"

Katie gasped. "Suzanne, you do not wish that! You do not wish that at all!"

Suzanne stared at Katie with surprise. "What's wrong with you?" she asked her.

Oops. Katie didn't know what to say. She hadn't meant to get so upset. It was just that Katie hated wishes.

That was because she knew how much trouble they could cause if they came true.

Chapter 2

It had all started one horrible day back in third grade. First, Katie had missed the football and lost the game for her team. Then she'd fallen in the mud and ruined her new jeans. Worst of all, she'd let out a giant burp right in front of the whole class. The kids had really teased her about that. Especially George. And he could be a really bad teaser.

It had definitely been one of the most embarrassing days of Katie's whole life. And that night, Katie wished she could be anyone but herself. There must have been a shooting star flying overhead when Katie made her wish, because the very next day the magic wind came.

The magic wind was unlike any wind Katie had ever seen before. It was a wild, fierce tornado that only blew around Katie.

But the worst part came after the wind *stopped* blowing. That's when the magic wind turned Katie into someone else. One . . . two . . . switcheroo!

The magic wind could turn Katie into anyone. The first time it appeared, it changed her into Speedy, the hamster in her third grade classroom. Katie spent the whole morning going around and around on a hamster wheel, and chewing on Speedy's wooden chew sticks. *Blech!* They tasted worse than the food in the school cafeteria!

Another time the magic wind came and turned Katie into Jeremy. That had been really awful. Katie hadn't known whether to go into the boys' room or the girls' room. She was really lucky she didn't have an accident that day!

Katie knew she would never forget when the magic wind showed up during her family vacation in Europe. That was when it turned Katie into an Italian gondola driver! Suddenly it was her job to paddle a boatload of people through the little canals in Venice.

Unfortunately, Katie didn't know her way around Venice. She didn't speak Italian either. Katie wound up getting everybody really, *really* lost. *Mamma mia!* What a mess that had been!

The magic wind was the reason Katie hated wishes so much. But of course she couldn't explain that to Suzanne. Her best friend probably wouldn't believe her even if she did. Katie wouldn't have believed it either, if it didn't keep happening to her.

Still, Katie knew she had to say something. Suzanne was staring at her.

"I just meant that you should learn to ignore Becky," Katie explained finally. "She's not going to go away. So you have to deal with her."

"I don't *have* to do anything," Suzanne answered.

Just then one of the teachers blew a loud whistle.

"Yes, you do," Katie told Suzanne. "You have to go inside. School's about to start."

"Okay, I guess I have to do that," Suzanne admitted. "But I don't have to sit near Becky in class. And I don't have to talk to her either."

There was no way the 4B teacher, Ms. Sweet, was going to let Suzanne ignore Becky all day. Sooner or later Suzanne would have to talk to her. But that didn't mean Suzanne was going to be nice when she did.

Today, more than ever, Katie was really glad she was in class 4A.

Chapter 3

Katie had *lots* of reasons to be glad she was in class 4A. Her teacher, Mr. Guthrie, was always surprising his class with cool and exciting things to do. And today was no exception!

As Katie walked up to the door of class 4A, she noticed something really weird. It was dark inside the classroom. All the window shades were drawn tight.

It was almost impossible for Katie to see anything. But once her eyes got used to the darkness, Katie realized that Mr. G had done something amazing to the room. He'd turned it into a dark, secret, animal world.

Well, not real animals. They were actually stuffed animals. But the room looked cool just the same. There were raccoons and opossums hiding near the trash can. A black-and-white skunk sat on the windowsill. A plastic owl with glow-in-the-dark eyes was perched on the branches of a fake tree near the chalkboard. And several rubber bats were hanging upside down from the light fixtures on the ceiling.

Seeing her classroom changed like this didn't seem weird to Katie at all. Mr. G was always decorating class 4A in fun ways.

What *was* weird, though, was the fact that Mr. G was nowhere to be found. Usually Katie's teacher greeted the kids as they walked into the room. But not today. The kids didn't see him anywhere.

"Hey, where's Mr. G?" Andy Epstein wondered out loud.

"Do you think he's absent?" Emma Stavros asked.

"I doubt it," Kevin answered her. "No

substitute would have done all this to our classroom."

"That's true," Emma S. agreed. "This is definitely a Mr. G room."

Mandy Banks picked up one of the stuffed raccoons. "What do you think this all means?" she wondered.

Katie looked up at the bats hanging from the ceiling. "Maybe it's for a Halloween party," she suggested. "I saw toy bats just like those in the Halloween section of the Party Palace store."

"But Halloween's not for two weeks, Katie Kazoo," George said, using the way-cool nickname he'd given her back in third grade.

"It's kind of creepy just standing here in the dark with no teacher," Emma Weber said.

"Maybe we should turn a light on," Andy suggested.

Bam! Just then the closet door swung open.

"AAAAHHHHH!" The kids all screamed at once.

Then they began to laugh. Their teacher had

12

just burst out of the closet. He was wearing gray and pink mouse ears on his head and a long gray tail on his behind.

"Mr. G!" Emma Weber shouted. "You scared me."

"Not me," George said. He was laughing really hard. "Why are you dressed like that?"

Kevin Camilleri walked over toward the light switch. But before he could flip it, Mr. G stopped him.

"Don't turn on the lights," Mr. G told Kevin. "Mice like me are happiest in the dark. So are opossums, skunks, bats, and raccoons. Too much light hurts our eyes."

"I think I know what this is all about," Katie said suddenly. "We're studying animals that come out in the dark."

"Very good, Katie," Mr. G told her. "They're called nocturnal animals."

Katie knew all about nocturnal animals because she had once *been* a nocturnal animal. One time at summer camp, the magic wind had turned her into a raccoon.

But of course Katie couldn't tell Mr. G that. So she said, "I already know raccoons are happiest in the dark."

"They sure are," Mr. G said. "All nocturnal animals are more active in the nighttime than in the daytime."

"Can we get started decorating our beanbags?" Emma W. asked Mr. G excitedly.

"Yep," Mr. G agreed. "Go to it!"

Decorating her beanbag chair was one of the things Katie loved best about being in Mr. G's class. The kids in 4A didn't sit at desks like other kids. They sat on beanbags. Mr. G thought kids learned better when they were comfortable.

Every time the class started a new learning adventure, they got to decorate their beanbag chairs with the craft supplies Mr. G kept in bags and boxes in the back of the classroom. Katie was using construction paper and streamers to turn her beanbag into a big raccoon.

Emma W. dotted her beanbag with pieces of shiny wrapping paper. "They're fireflies," she explained to Katie. "They only come out at night."

George used black-and-white construction paper to turn his beanbag into a giant skunk. Then he took off his sneakers and began rubbing them all over his beanbag chair.

"Dude, what are you doing?" Mr. G asked George.

"Making my beanbag smell," George answered. "My sneakers stink as bad as any real skunk."

"That's the truth," Kevin agreed.

Mr. G laughed. "How about we just *pretend*

your beanbag skunk smells?" he suggested. "Put your sneakers back on. You're going to need them in a few minutes. We're going outside to play a special game."

Katie grinned. They were going to get to go outside and run around, and it wasn't even gym class!

One thing was for sure. Class 4A was the best place to be . . . day or night!

Chapter 4

"We're so lucky," Katie said to Emma W. as the girls walked outside with the rest of the kids in class 4A. "Everyone else at school is inside doing work, and we're out here."

"I know," Emma W. agreed. "I wonder what kind of game we're going to play."

The girls didn't have to wait long to find out. A minute later, Mr. G stood in front of the class. He was holding a blindfold.

"Today we're playing a game called Bat and Bugs," Mr. G told the kids. "One of you will be a bat, and the rest of you will be mosquitoes. The trick is for the bat to catch as many mosquitoes as he can."

"Oh, it's just like tag," Kadeem Carter said.

"Sort of," Mr. G said. "Except the person who is doing the tagging is blindfolded."

The kids all stared at their teacher. That didn't make any sense at all.

"How is the bat supposed to find the mosquitoes if she's blindfolded?" Mandy Banks asked Mr. G.

"With echolocation," Mr. G replied.

"Echo what?" George asked.

"Echolocation," Mr. G said again. "That's how bats catch their food in the wild. Bats don't see very well. So they make sounds to help them find food."

"Okay, that makes no sense at all," George said.

"It makes a lot of sense," Mr. G assured him. "In fact bats use their *best* sense when they use echolocation."

"What's a bat's best sense?" Katie asked.

"Good question, Katie," Mr. G said.

Katie smiled proudly. She knew Mr. G

thought that asking good questions was really, really important. He said it was how kids learned.

"Bats have a very strong sense of hearing. It's more powerful than their eyesight," Mr. G told the class. "So when bats are looking for food, they send out sound waves using their mouth or nose. When the sound hits an object, an echo comes back. The bat can tell what kind of object it is by the sound of the echo. They can even tell the size, shape, and texture of a tiny insect!"

"So in the game the person who is the bat has to send out a sound?" Andy asked.

"Exactly," Mr. G agreed. "And all the mosquitoes have to send back the same sound. They *echo* the bat. Then the bat moves in the direction of the sounds. The *echoes* tell him the *location* of the mosquitoes. Echolocation."

"Cool!" George said. "Can I be the bat first?"

"Sure," Mr. G said. "Come on up and put the blindfold on."

A minute later, the blindfolded George-the-bat was running, searching for the mosquitoes.

"*Blurp*," George shouted out.

"*Blurp*," the kids echoed back.

"*Gleep*," George called out.

"*Gleep*," the kids echoed back again.

Katie giggled as she watched George trying to catch some "mosquitoes." His arms were flailing all around as he tried to catch his friends.

"*Shloop!*" George-the-bat screamed.

Katie laughed even harder. She doubted real bats made such goofy noises. But George's silly sounds were making the game even more fun.

"*Shloop!*" Katie-the-mosquito yelled back happily.

Katie would *not* have been happy if the magic wind had come and switcherooed her into a real mosquito. She didn't think stinging people would be much fun. And getting squooshed? Horrible.

But the magic wind was nowhere near her.

And Katie wasn't a real mosquito. She was just a *pretend* mosquito.

"*Veloorp,*" George called.

"*Veloorp!*" Katie echoed back at the top of her lungs.

"I hear Katie Kazoo!" George shouted. He started running toward the sound of her voice.

"I hear Katie Kazoo!" Katie shouted back to him.

Then she ducked down so George missed grabbing her. She didn't want a bat—even a make-believe bat like George—to catch her today!

Chapter 5

"I don't know how you guys learn anything in your class," Suzanne said to Katie, George, and Kevin. It was Saturday morning. A bunch of the fourth-graders had come to Katie's house to bake animal cookies. "All you ever do is play games."

"We learn a lot," Katie told Suzanne. Everyone was sitting at the kitchen table, lining up bowls and measuring spoons and all the stuff for baking cookies. "And we're going to prove it to you when we all go to the zoo on Monday. Our class is going to tell your class about the nocturnal animals."

"Well, *we're* going to tell *you* about the

animals that are awake during the daytime," Suzanne said. "And we're going to have lots of information. We spent the whole morning in the school library yesterday."

"We spent the morning out on the field," George said.

"That's what I mean," Suzanne continued. "What can you learn on a field?"

"Actually, we learned all about bats and echolocation," Katie told her.

"What's that?" Becky asked Katie.

Katie handed Kevin the flour from one of the cabinets. She opened her mouth to answer Becky. But Suzanne butted in before she could say a word.

"Who cares what it is?" Suzanne said. "The class 4B kids definitely have the better animals to study. While your class is stuck learning about yucky night animals like bats, we're learning about cute day animals."

"That's true," Becky said. "Like horses. They're my favorite!"

"We know," Suzanne said, rolling her eyes. "You're always talking about your horseback riding lessons—when you're not talking about gymnastics, that is."

Katie frowned. Obviously, Suzanne was still mad about what had happened on the monkey bars yesterday.

"Well at least I'm good at something," Becky said. "I have medals for gymnastics and ribbons for my horseback riding."

"Oh yeah?" Suzanne started. "Well I . . ."

"Speaking of horses," George butted in. "Do you guys know what it means when you find a horseshoe?"

"What?" Kevin asked.

"It means some horse is walking around in just his socks!" George answered. Then he started laughing at his own joke.

Ding-dong. Just then the doorbell rang.

"I'll get it," Mrs. Carew told the kids. "You guys keep on measuring that flour."

"Will do, Mom," Katie said.

A few seconds later the kids heard Katie's mom say, "Hi, Jeremy. You're just in time to help mix the dough."

"Great," Jeremy said. "I came here as soon as my soccer game was over."

Katie was really glad Jeremy had shown up to be part of the cooking club this week. But she wasn't nearly as happy as Becky was.

"Jeremy!" Becky squealed. "You're here!" Then she raised up her arms, and flipped over.

It was a perfect back handspring—until Becky's foot tapped the table leg, knocking off the bag of flour.

"Hey!" George shouted out as a stream of white flour poured onto his black jeans.

"Whoops," Becky said as she stood up straight. "Sorry about that."

George looked down at his black-and-white legs and frowned. Then, suddenly he smiled. "Do you guys know what's black and white with red dots?" he asked the kids.

"What?" Katie asked him.

"A zebra with chicken pox!" George said. He started laughing again.

Katie, Jeremy, Becky, and Kevin all laughed, too. But Suzanne wasn't in the mood to laugh. She was in the mood to be angry with Becky.

"Now that Becky's spilled all the flour, what are we supposed to use for our cookies?" Suzanne asked.

"Don't worry," Katie's mom told Suzanne. "I have another bag."

"I'll clean up the mess, Mrs. Carew," Becky said. "Where's the broom?"

"In the closet," Mrs. Carew said, pointing toward the broom closet in the corner of the room.

"I told you Becky was a show-off," Suzanne whispered to Katie. Only her whisper wasn't a quiet whisper. It was a loud one. Suzanne wanted to make sure Becky heard her.

Katie couldn't take it anymore. She had to get away from Suzanne and Becky, and all the fighting. So she headed off toward the living room.

"Where are you going, Katie Kazoo?" George asked her.

"To the computer," Katie told him. "I want to go on the Cherrydale Zoo website. I'm going to make cookies that look like nocturnal animals. I want to print out some pictures."

"Good idea," Kevin said. "Can you print out a picture of a raccoon for me?"

"Sure," Katie told him.

While Becky cleaned up, and the other kids began to mix the batter, Katie went on to the zoo website. As soon as the animal pictures popped up on her screen, Katie began to smile.

"Wow!" she exclaimed. "This is sooooo cool!"

"What is?" Suzanne shouted. She ran into the living room.

So did all the other kids. They wanted to know what Katie was so excited about.

Chapter 6

The kids were staring at the computer screen.

"What's the big deal?" Kevin asked Katie.

"Look!" Katie answered. "The zoo is giving people the chance to adopt an animal."

Just then, Katie's dog Pepper came running into the room. He raced over to Katie and rubbed his little brown and white cocker spaniel body against her jeans.

Katie bent down and scratched his chin. "Don't worry, Pepper," she said. "I don't mean I would adopt a tiger and bring him home. If you adopt a zoo animal, the animal stays at the zoo."

"How do you adopt an animal if it doesn't live with you?" George asked.

Katie scrolled down a little on the screen. "See, it explains it all here," Katie told him. "You can donate money to the zoo to help care for an animal. Then the zoo sends you pictures of your animal, and information about him. Best of all, you get to name the animal."

The other kids didn't seem nearly as excited as Katie did.

"Nobody loves animals the way you do, Katie," Jeremy said. "Are you going to do it?"

Katie shook her head. "I can't. It costs

twenty dollars to adopt a zoo animal," she said. "I only have seven dollars of my birthday money left."

"That's too bad," Jeremy told her. "It would have been a really nice thing to do. That's what I like about you, Katie. You're always so nice."

Becky turned and looked at Jeremy for a minute. Then she smiled at Katie. "I have some of my birthday money left," she said. "Maybe we could adopt an animal together."

"Wow!" Katie exclaimed. "You would do that?"

"Sure," Becky told her. "I'm nice, too." She grinned at Jeremy.

Jeremy blushed. He pushed his glasses up on his nose and stared at the floor.

"Thanks," Katie said to Becky. "How much do you have?"

"Six dollars," Becky said.

Katie frowned. "That only makes thirteen dollars. It's still not enough."

"I'm broke or I would chip in," Kevin told

Katie and Becky. "It's really cool that you guys want to help a zoo animal."

Suzanne had heard enough. "Oh, please. They're not the only ones who want to help animals. I'm nice, too!" she exclaimed. "In fact, I'm going to donate seven dollars that my aunt gave me last Christmas."

"Wow! Suzanne, that *is* nice of you," George said. He sounded surprised.

Suzanne smiled sweetly at George. Well, as sweetly as Suzanne could smile, anyway. "I know," she told him.

Katie thought for a minute. "I have seven dollars. Becky has six. And now with Suzanne's seven dollars, we have twenty dollars! That's just enough. We did it!"

"Yay!" Becky shouted.

"Once again, I saved the day," Suzanne reminded Becky and Katie.

Katie laughed. That was such a Suzanne thing to say. But it was also true.

"What animal should we adopt?" Becky

wondered. "How about a monkey? I love the way they swing from tree to tree."

"I'd rather adopt a peacock," Suzanne suggested. "They're so elegant and pretty."

"A peacock?" Becky asked her. "They're too fancy. And they always look kind of snobby to me."

"Why don't we adopt an animal that's not so cute or pretty?" Katie suggested. "Like a rhinoceros."

Becky and Suzanne both stared at her.

"Why would we want to do that?" Suzanne asked.

"Because no one else would want to," Katie explained. "Cute monkeys or beautiful birds will always get someone to adopt them. But animals that aren't so cute need to be adopted, too."

"You didn't feel that way when you adopted Pepper," Suzanne said. "You told me he was the cutest animal at the Cherrydale Animal Shelter."

"He was," Katie admitted. "Pepper was a really adorable puppy. But I think a baby rhinoceros could be cute, too."

"To who?" Becky asked her.

Katie thought about that for a minute. "I guess to a mommy rhinoceros," she said finally.

"I don't want to adopt a rhinoceros," Suzanne said. "They're too ugly with those weird horns and their thick skin. What about a flamingo? They're that gorgeous pink color. I've always looked pretty in pink."

"So go to the mall and buy a dress," Becky said. "I want to adopt a cuddly animal."

"You don't get to *hold* the animal, Becky," Suzanne said.

Grrrr. Katie couldn't stand it any more. No matter what was going on, Suzanne and Becky just kept fighting about it.

"Look you guys, we don't have to decide this today," she said finally. "The whole fourth grade is going to the zoo on Monday. We can check out the animals there, and then decide."

"Maybe seeing them in person will help you pick the right animal," Jeremy told the girls.

"I'm sure you're right, Jeremy," Becky cooed. "You're so smart."

Jeremy rolled his eyes and turned away from her.

"Can we go bake some cookies now?" Kevin asked. "This is supposed to be a cooking club, remember?"

"Yeah!" George agreed. "I'm going to make one cookie shaped like a peacock, one shaped like a monkey, and one shaped like a rhino. I like them all the same—especially when they're sprinkled with sugar!"

Katie giggled. That was soooo George. No matter what the problem, he could always solve it with dessert.

If only her problems with Becky and Suzanne could be solved that easily!

Chapter 7

Unfortunately, Suzanne and Becky were still fighting when the fourth grade arrived at the zoo on Monday morning.

"I hope we go to the monkey house first," Becky said. "I want to see if we can find a really cute one to adopt."

"I told you, we're *not* adopting a monkey," Suzanne insisted. "Right, Katie?"

Katie didn't know what to say. So she didn't answer.

Suzanne twirled around, showing off her bright blue shirt and blue and green skirt. "I dressed this way so our peacock will know I'm the one who's adopting her," Suzanne said.

"The three of us are adopting a zoo animal together," Katie reminded Suzanne.

"Of course," Suzanne said. "But *I* look the most like a peacock mom."

"Actually, Suzanne, you look like a peacock *dad*," Jeremy corrected her. "The boys are the colorful ones."

"That can't be right," Suzanne insisted.

"Jeremy is right, Suzanne," Ms. Sweet said. "Very often female birds have duller colors than males. They can fade into their environment while they are sitting on the nest. It keeps the females and their eggs safe."

"The females are pea*hens*," Mr. G added. "The male birds are the peacocks."

"Ha ha ha! Suzanne's dressed like a *boy* bird!" Becky giggled.

George laughed along with her. "Suzanne's more of a pea *brain* than a peacock," he whispered to Kevin.

Katie was walking next to George. She heard what he said. Usually she hated when George said something mean about one of her friends. But today she was feeling kind of angry with Suzanne and Becky, too. So, she didn't tell him not to say things like that.

"Have you thought more about what kind of animal you want to adopt, Katie?" Becky asked.

Suzanne rolled her eyes. "Katie probably wants a nocturnal animal. Something gross from the Cave of Darkness exhibit, like a scorpion or a bat."

Katie shook her head. "No thanks. Bats are too creepy. Even for me."

"I don't blame you, Katie Kazoo," Kevin said. "Who would want an animal that drinks blood?"

George raised his arms out wide like bat wings, and used his best vampire voice. "I vant to bite your neck! Blaaahhh!"

"Dude, that's just a myth," Mr. G told George. "There *are* vampire bats, but they don't suck the blood from people's necks. They get their blood from cows and horses."

"Oh my!" Katie explained. "That's awful."

Mr. G shook his head. "The animals don't feel a thing," he assured Katie. "And the bats take very little of their blood. The animals aren't harmed at all."

Katie still looked a little afraid.

"Don't worry, Katie Kazoo," Mr. G assured her. "There are no vampire bats at this zoo."

Ms. Sweet clapped her hands. "Okay, boys and girls, gather 'round," she said. "Does everyone have a map of the zoo?"

The kids all held up the maps they had been given at the entrance.

"Terrific," Ms. Sweet continued. "I want you to stick with the group. But should you get lost, go straight to the help desk near the Monkey Jungle. Someone there will help you get back to the group."

"You see how great monkeys are?" Becky said to Suzanne. "The zoo put the help desk right next to their habitat."

"What does that prove?" Suzanne asked her.

Katie didn't wait for Becky's answer. She

moved to the back of the group near Emma
W. and Miriam Chan. Unfortunately, a few
minutes later Katie heard Suzanne and Becky
bickering again. Everybody could.

At the Elephant Trail, they argued over
which elephant had the biggest ears.

At the Penguin Iceberg, they argued over
which of the penguins had the funniest waddle.

At the Hippo Pool, they argued over which
hippo was fattest.

In the Owl House, they argued over which owl looked the smartest.

Finally, Ms. Sweet stepped in. "If you girls can't behave, you'll have to wait for us at the help desk," she warned Suzanne and Becky.

Katie was surprised. Ms. Sweet actually sounded angry. She never got angry. At least not that Katie had ever seen.

Apparently, Becky and Suzanne were surprised, too, because they got really quiet. The mention of the help desk reminded Katie of something. "My map!" she cried out suddenly.

"What happened, Katie?" Emma W. asked her.

"I left my zoo map at the Owl House," Katie told her. "I have to go get it."

"We can share mine," Emma W. told her.

Katie shook her head. "I wanted to bring mine home. The Owl House is just right over there. I'll run over and get it, and then catch up with you guys."

"Don't get lost, Katie," Mr. G called to her. "We're heading to the Hall of Lizards."

"I'll be right there," Katie called back. And with that, she hurried off as fast as she could. She didn't want to be gone too long.

Katie spotted her map on the bench just outside the Owl House. She bent over to pick it up, when suddenly she felt a cool wind blowing against her neck.

Feeling a cool breeze wasn't strange. After all, it was fall. The days were colder in the fall. The breeze got stronger. It was a wind now. And it didn't seem to be blowing anywhere but on the back of Katie's neck. The leaves in the trees weren't moving. Neither was the paper map on the bench.

Now *that* was strange.

It could only mean one thing. This was no ordinary wind. This was the magic wind!

"Oh no!" Katie shouted out. "Not now! Go away, magic wind!"

But the magic wind wouldn't go away. Instead it grew stronger and stronger, circling around Katie like a wild tornado. Katie shut her eyes tight and tried really hard not to cry.

And then it stopped. Just like that. The magic wind was gone.

And so was Katie Carew. She'd turned into someone else. One . . . two . . . switcheroo! But who?

Chapter 8

Where was she?

Katie blinked for a minute and then opened her eyes. But she might as well have kept them shut. It was so dark, she could barely see a thing. She wasn't outside the Owl House. That was for sure.

But she sure could hear a lot. All around her she heard all sorts off beeps and plings. She also heard what sounded like tiny footsteps and buzzing noises.

How weird was that?

And she had the funny feeling that she was hanging upside down—sort of like when she hung on the monkey bars at school.

Suddenly Katie noticed an itchy feeling just below her left wing. Carefully she unhooked one of her claws from the tree branch above her, and began to scratch at her soft, dark brown fur.

Whoa! Wait a minute. *Wings? Claws? Fur?*

There was only one animal that had both wings and fur, and hung upside down while it was resting. Oh no! The magic wind had changed Katie into a bat!

Katie was stuck in the dark, dismal Cave of Darkness! It was just her and the bats. Right now, Katie Kazoo was a creature of the night. How could she escape? Even with her bad bat-eyesight, she could see that she was trapped inside the exhibit area. There must be a door somewhere. But if she did escape, what then? She'd still be a bat flying around the zoo.

This was *soooo* not good.

And neither was the itchy feeling. Katie stretched her wing out a little farther to get a better scratch. Then she licked at her fur with her tongue. Mmm . . . it felt so good to groom herself.

The bat hanging next to her didn't seem to like what Katie was doing, though. Apparently, it didn't like being bumped into. It stretched out a wing and shoved Katie slightly.

"Hey!" Katie shouted. "You almost knocked me off my perch."

"Yeah, well, you hit me with your wing and woke me up," the other bat told Katie. "And I like my beauty rest."

"Oh. I'm sorry," Katie apologized. "I just had an itch."

Of course, Katie's apology didn't sound like words at all. It sounded more like *ping . . . ping . . . ping* noises.

And a moment later, those same sounds echoed back to Katie. From the sound of the echoes, Katie could tell that there were some tasty mosquitoes flying by.

Tasty mosquitoes. Now there were two words Katie never thought she'd say in the same sentence. For one thing, Katie was a vegetarian. And for another, mosquitoes were bugs. Who would want to eat a bug?

A bat. That's who!

Katie pushed off from her perch and began to flap her wings. Wow! How cool was this? She was flying!

As she soared through the dark cave, Katie opened her little bat mouth and let out a pinging noise. A moment later it echoed back. Now Katie knew exactly where that mosquito was.

Dinnertime! Katie swooped down and swallowed the bug whole.

Soon Katie was joined by several other bats, each sending out their own sounds in search of food. She had to admit it was kind of fun, just flying around in the dark, catching bugs.

Then, suddenly behind her a flash of light pierced the darkness. Katie turned. The light hurt her eyes. Someone had opened the back door into the exhibit area. Was it a zookeeper? Or was it someone more dangerous?

Chapter 9

"It's your fault we got sent to the help desk," the someone said angrily.

Katie listened carefully to the high-pitched, loud voice. *Definitely not a zookeeper,* she thought.

"This is not the help desk," a second human voice said.

Katie gulped. There were two people inside the bat exhibit. Who were they?

"Obviously," the first voice answered sarcastically. "We made a wrong turn."

Suddenly, Katie realized she knew *that* voice really, really well. "Suzanne!" she shouted out.

But all Katie's best friend heard was "Squeak!" After all, Katie was a bat now.

"Did you hear that?" the second someone said.

Katie's bat-mouth broke into a large grin. That slow, southern accent had to belong to Becky. The two someones weren't big, bad predators. They were just fourth-grade girls!

Katie was soooo happy to know that there were no predators in the cave with her, it made her want to fly!

"Whee!" Katie squealed excitedly. She did a joyful loop-the-loop in the air, and caught a passing mosquito in her teeth.

"AAAAHHHHH!" Suzanne and Becky cried out at once. "A bat!"

Oops. Katie hadn't meant to scare her friends. She'd just wanted to show them how happy she was to see them.

"We're inside the bat exhibit," Becky shouted.

"Not for long. I'm getting out of here!" Suzanne said. Then she stopped for a minute and

looked around. "Um . . . where's the door?" she
asked.

"I don't know," Becky said. "I'm all turned
around."

Katie understood why the girls couldn't find
the door. The back wall was painted floor to
ceiling with pictures of cave rocks and flying
bats. It made it impossible to see where the door
was in the wall.

"I can't believe you got us stuck in here!"
Suzanne yelled at Becky.

"I did not," Becky answered. "In fact, *I* was following *you*."

"Well, who asked you to?" Suzanne shouted back.

"Ms. Sweet," Becky reminded her. "She said we had to stick together. And you said you knew how to read the zoo map."

"Yeah, well, this is no big deal," Suzanne told her.

"No big deal?" Becky demanded. "Are you kidding? We're stuck in here with a bunch of creepy, dirty bats."

Now Katie was the one who was mad. She wasn't creepy. And she certainly wasn't dirty. She'd just groomed herself.

"Relax," Suzanne told Becky. "As soon as a zookeeper comes in here to take care of the bats, the door will open. That's when we'll leave."

"What if the zookeeper doesn't show up until tomorrow?" Becky asked. "We could be stuck in here overnight."

"Don't say that, Becky!" Suzanne shouted.

All this arguing was getting to Katie. She perched upside down and pulled her wings tight over her ears to block out the loud voices. But it didn't help. Her sensitive bat ears were picking up every sound.

It was amazing. It didn't matter where Katie went or who she switcherooed into. Suzanne and Becky's battles followed her everywhere!

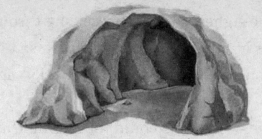

Chapter 10

Katie wasn't the only one getting a headache. She could tell by the way the other bats were squeaking that Suzanne and Becky were scaring them.

Katie tried making noises to tell the other bats not to be afraid of her friends. But they didn't believe her.

"We don't like when non-bats come in here," one bat told Katie.

"Except that zookeeper human," another bat said. "Sometimes she brings tasty insect treats for us to snack on."

"Well, these aren't zookeeper humans," the first bat insisted. "They're regular humans."

Katie sighed. She wasn't getting through to the bats at all. And she knew she wasn't going to be able to calm Suzanne and Becky's fears either.

Katie wished she could tell Suzanne and Becky that bats were cool. They were great flyers—better than birds even. And the whole echolocation thing worked really well. There was never any problem finding food. But there was no way Katie could explain that to them right now. Becky and Suzanne didn't speak bat.

But Katie did. And right now, one of the bats was yelling at her.

"We have to get those two humans out of here!" the bat squeaked angrily.

"I know," Katie agreed in bat-speak. "But they can't find the way out."

"I'm right by the door," the bat told her. "Just get them over here."

How was Katie supposed to do that? She couldn't just lead them there. Suzanne and Becky would never follow a bat. They would run away from her instead.

That was it!

Suddenly, Katie got one of her great ideas! If she couldn't *lead* the girls to the door, she would have to *scare* them there!

All Katie had to do was keep flying behind Becky and Suzanne. They'd try and run away from her. Eventually, Katie would force them to run in the direction of the door.

"Ping! Ping! Ping!" Katie let out a few high-pitched sounds.

Ping! Ping! Ping! The sounds echoed right back, letting Katie know exactly where Suzanne and Becky were standing. She took off and flew right for the girls.

"Aaaahhhhh!" Becky and Suzanne cried out. They began to run.

Their loud squeals hurt Katie's sensitive ears. But she refused to let that stop her. She had a job to do, and she was going to do it!

"Move, move!" she squealed.

Ping. Ping. The sounds echoed back.

"Aaahhh!" Becky screamed.

"Stay out of my hair!" Suzanne added as she ran away from Katie.

The plan was working! Becky and Suzanne were moving quickly toward the side of the cave where the door was. Katie could tell by the echoing sound of their footsteps.

"Did you find the door yet?" Becky asked Suzanne nervously.

"Not yet," Suzanne told her. "But I'm running my hands along the wall. Sooner or later I've got to hit a doorknob."

"I sure hope it's sooner," Becky answered her.

"I found the door!" Suzanne yelled out suddenly.

"Open it! Fast," Becky told her.

Suzanne did just that. A moment later a burst of light flooded the dark bat exhibit. Katie's bat-eyes squinted. Instinctively, she flew off to a dark corner.

"Let's get out of here!" Suzanne shouted.

"Right behind you," Becky agreed.

"*Au revoir*," a bat called out to the girls as they left the cave.

Katie's bat-eyes opened wide. Who knew bats could speak French?

Katie heard the sounds of footsteps rushing out the door. Then Katie heard the door closing. The cave was dark again. Suzanne and Becky were gone.

Katie was happy for her friends. They were back outside where they belonged.

But she was also sad for herself. Yes, being

a bat was fun. But she was ready to turn back into herself again.

Yawn. Suddenly Katie felt very tired. All that flying, eating, and chasing had taken a lot out of her. She flew over to a nearby tree, hooked her feet on a thick branch, and flipped over for a well deserved, upside-down nap.

But no sooner did Katie shut her bat-eyes, than she felt a cool breeze blowing on the back of her wings.

She wondered if any of the other bats felt air rushing into the cave. But they all seemed perfectly fine, hanging there, upside down.

This wind seemed to be blowing only on Katie. And that could mean only one thing. This was no ordinary wind. This was the magic wind.

The magic wind picked up speed then, swirling and whirling around Katie so hard that she thought her little bat body might be blown away. She gripped the branch hard with her claws and held on tight.

And then it stopped. Just like that. The magic wind was gone, and Katie was back.

Thud! Katie fell to the ground and landed on her rear end. Red sneakers could not grip tree branches the way bat claws did. But that was okay. She was just glad to be back to herself again.

Quickly, she ran her hands along the walls of the cave until she found the doorknob. As soon as she did, she opened the door and raced outside.

"Bye!" she called back to the bats, hoping they understood.

Chapter 11

Katie wasn't afraid of the bats anymore. But she was worried about what was going to happen when her teacher realized she'd wandered off. Mr. G wasn't going to like that. Not one bit.

Uh-oh. Just then she saw Mr. G coming toward her.

"Katie, there you are!" Mr. G exclaimed. Luckily, he sounded more relieved than mad. "I was wondering what had happened to you."

"I . . . um . . . I went back to get my map, and I got all lost and wound up here," Katie told him.

That was the truth, *sort of*. She'd just left out the whole part about the magic wind and turning into a bat.

"Oh," Mr. G replied. "Well, I'm glad we found you. I'm just sorry you missed the Hall of Lizards. I know you would have liked the chameleons."

"I'm really sorry," Katie apologized. "I didn't mean to end up at the bat cave."

Now *that* was definitely the truth.

"Well, we found you just in time," Mr. G told her. "I'm glad you won't miss this exhibit. After all, you're one of our fourth-grade bat experts."

Katie grinned. She was a bat expert all right. More than Mr. G would ever know!

★ ★ ★

A little while later, Katie was sitting on the bus heading back to school with her friends. She was really tired from all the flying. But it had also been fun. And it had helped her make an important decision.

"Hey, you guys, I think I know what animal

we should adopt," Katie told Suzanne and Becky.

"Which one?" Suzanne asked.

Katie took a deep breath. She had a feeling her friends weren't going to like this. "A bat. A little brown bat."

"Oooh, gross!" Becky shouted. "I hate bats."

"I don't like them, either," Suzanne said.

Katie sighed. Finally her friends were agreeing on something. But it didn't make Katie happy.

"Ouch!" Suzanne exclaimed. She started scratching the red bumps on both her arms. "I'm like a mosquito magnet. Look how many bites I got last night."

"Bats eat mosquitoes. Did you know that?" Katie asked Suzanne. "So you should be grateful to bats."

"Um . . . I guess so," Suzanne murmured.

"A bat would be a great animal to adopt," Jeremy told the girls. "There are bat heroes, like Batman."

Becky turned to Jeremy. "Do you really think we should adopt a bat?" she asked him as she batted her eyes and smiled.

Jeremy blushed red and shrugged. "Sure. Why not?"

"Then I think we should adopt a bat," Becky said.

Suzanne rolled her eyes. But a moment later she said, "Okay, a bat it is. This whole adoption thing was Katie's idea anyway. She should get to pick. And bats are kind of graceful when they fly."

Katie laughed and sat back in her seat. She was happy that they had all finally agreed on a zoo animal to adopt. Everything was peaceful again.

But not for long.

"I think we should name our brown bat Batly," Becky said.

"That's a dumb name," Suzanne told her. "In fact, it's not even a name."

"Well what name were you thinking of?"

Becky asked Suzanne.

"Aurora," Suzanne answered. "Like the princess in *Sleeping Beauty*. Because bats sleep in the daytime."

"But they're awake at night," Becky said. "And who ever heard of naming a bat after a princess, anyway?"

"Here we go again," Katie said to Jeremy.

"Those two will never change," Jeremy agreed.

Katie smiled. She was actually glad about that. With all the changes and switcheroos she kept going through, it was good to know that some things would always be the same.

Chapter 12

Bat Facts!

Being switcherooed into a bat taught Katie a whole lot about what bats are really like. Luckily, you don't have to wait for a magic wind to turn you into a bat to become a bat expert. There are plenty of cool bat facts right here!

⭐ Bats are the only mammals that can fly.

⭐ Bats are ancient animals that have been around at least fifty million years.

★ One of the world's smallest mammals is the bumblebee bat from Thailand. It weighs less than a penny!

★ The giant flying fox bats of Indonesia have wings that stretch out as far as six feet— that's how tall many adult men are!

★ The brown myotis bat can catch more than one thousand mosquitoes in an hour—often two in a second!

★ Vampire bats adopt orphan bats. They've been known to risk their own lives to share food with the less fortunate bats.

★ Honduran white bats cut large leaves to make "tents" that protect their colonies from jungle rains.

★ There are nearly one thousand different

species of bats. Most of them are so small they could fit in the palm of your hand.

⭐ African heart-nosed bats can hear the footsteps of a beetle walking on sand six feet away!

About the Author

Nancy Krulik is the author of more than 150 books for children and young adults, including three *New York Times* best sellers. She lives in New York City with her husband, composer Daniel Burwasser, their children, Amanda and Ian, and Pepper, a chocolate and white spaniel mix. When she's not busy writing the *Katie Kazoo, Switcheroo* series, Nancy loves swimming, reading, and going to the movies.

★ ★ ★

About the Illustrators

John & Wendy have illustrated all of the *Katie Kazoo* books, but when they're not busy drawing Katie and her friends, they like to paint, take photographs, travel, and play music in their rock 'n' roll band. They live and work in Brooklyn, New York.